THE CHRISTMAS STORY

THE CHRIST-MAS STORY from

the Gospels of Matthew & Luke

Edited by Marguerite Northrup

THE METROPOLITAN
MUSEUM OF ART *Distributed*
by New York Graphic Society, *Greenwich, Connecticut*

The selections from the Gospels are from
the King James Version of the Bible

Copyright 1950 by Pantheon Books Inc.
Copyright © 1966 by The Metropolitan Museum of Art
Third printing, 1972
Library of Congress catalog card number 65-23504
International Standard Book Number 0-87099-047-0

For unto us a child is born,

unto us a son is given:

and the government

shall be upon his shoulder:

and his name shall be called

Wonderful, Counsellor,

The mighty God,

The everlasting Father,

The Prince of Peace.

ISAIAH 9:6

THERE was in the days of Herod, the king of Judaea, a certain priest named Zacharias, of the course of Abia: and his wife was of the daughters of Aaron, and her name was Elisabeth. And they were both righteous before God, walking in all the commandments and ordinances of the Lord blameless. And they had no child, because that Elisabeth was barren, and they both were now well stricken in years. And there appeared unto him an angel of the Lord standing on the right side of the altar of incense. And when Zacharias saw him, he was troubled, and fear fell upon him. But the angel said unto him, Fear not, Zacharias: for thy prayer is heard; and thy wife Elisabeth shall bear thee a son, and thou shalt call his name John. And thou shalt have joy and gladness; and many shall rejoice at his birth. And Zacharias said unto the angel, Whereby shall I know this? for I am an old man, and my wife well stricken in years. And the angel answering said unto him, I am Gabriel, that stand in the presence of God; and am sent to speak unto thee, and to shew thee these glad tidings.  And, behold, thou shalt be dumb, and not able to speak, until the day that these things shall be performed, because thou believest not my words, which shall be fulfilled in their season. And the people waited for Zacharias, and marvelled that he tarried so long in the temple. And when he came out, he could not speak unto them: and they perceived that he had seen a vision in the temple: for he beckoned unto them, and remained speechless. And it came to pass, that, as soon as the days of his ministration were accomplished, he departed to his own house. And after those days his wife Elisabeth conceived, and hid herself five months, saying, Thus hath the Lord dealt with me in the days wherein he looked on me, to take away my reproach among men.

ND in the sixth month the angel Gabriel was sent from God unto a city of Galilee, named Nazareth, To a virgin espoused to a man whose name was Joseph, of the house of David; and the virgin's name was Mary. And the angel came in unto her, and said, Hail, thou that art highly favoured, the Lord is with thee: blessed art thou among women. And when she saw him, she was troubled at his saying, and cast in her mind what manner of salutation this should be. And the angel said unto her, Fear not, Mary: for thou hast found favour with God. And, behold, thou shalt conceive in thy womb, and bring forth a son, and shalt call his name JESUS. He shall be great, and shall be called the Son of the Highest: and the Lord God shall give unto him the throne of his father David: And he shall reign over the house of Jacob for ever; and of his kingdom there shall be no end.

8

T H E N said Mary unto the angel, How shall this be, seeing I know not a man? And the angel answered and said unto her, The Holy Ghost shall come upon thee, and the power of the Highest shall overshadow thee: therefore also that holy thing which shall be born of thee shall be called the Son of God. And, behold, thy cousin Elisabeth, she hath also conceived a son in her old age: and this is the sixth month with her, who was called barren. For with God nothing shall be impossible. And Mary said, Behold the handmaid of the Lord; be it unto me according to thy word. And the angel departed from her.

The Annunciation (detail)
by Robert Campin

11

The Visitation by a follower of
Rogier van der Weyden

A N D Mary arose in those days, and went into the hill country with haste, into a city of Juda; And entered into the house of Zacharias, and saluted Elisabeth. And it came to pass, that, when Elisabeth heard the salutation of Mary, the babe leaped in her womb; and Elisabeth was filled with the Holy Ghost: And she spake out with a loud voice, and said, Blessed art thou among women, and blessed is the fruit of thy womb. And whence is this to me, that the mother of my Lord should come to me? For, lo, as soon as the voice of thy salutation sounded in mine ears, the babe leaped in my womb for joy. And blessed is she that believed: for there shall be a performance of those things which were told her from the Lord. And Mary said, My soul doth magnify the Lord, And my spirit hath rejoiced in God my Saviour. For he hath regarded the low estate of his handmaiden: for, behold, from henceforth all generations shall call me blessed. For he that is mighty hath done to me great things; and holy is his name. And his mercy is on them that fear him from generation to generation. He hath shewed strength with his arm; he hath scattered the proud in the imagination of their hearts. He hath put down the mighty from their seats, and exalted them of low degree. He hath filled the hungry with good things; and the rich he hath sent empty away. He hath holpen his servant Israel, in remembrance of his mercy; As he spake to our fathers, to Abraham, and to his seed for ever. And Mary abode with her about three months, and returned to her own house.

AND it came to pass in those days, that there went out a decree from Caesar Augustus, that all the world should be taxed. And all went to be taxed, every one into his own city. And Joseph also went up from Galilee, out of the city of Nazareth, into Judaea, unto the city of David, which is called Bethlehem; (because he was of the house and lineage of David:) To be taxed with Mary his espoused wife, being great with child. And so it was, that, while they were there, the days were accomplished that she should be delivered. And she brought forth her firstborn son, and wrapped him in swaddling clothes, and laid him in a manger; because there was no room for them in the inn.

The Nativity by the workshop of Fra Angelico

AND there were in the same country shepherds abiding in the field, keeping watch over their flock by night. And, lo, the angel of the Lord came upon them, and the glory of the Lord shone round about them: and they were sore afraid. And the angel said unto them, Fear not: for, behold, I bring you good tidings of great joy, which shall be to all people. For unto you is born this day in the city of David a Saviour, which is Christ the Lord. And this shall be a sign unto you; Ye shall find the babe wrapped in swaddling clothes, lying in a manger.

A shepherd tending his flock
(detail) from The Nativity
by Antoniazzo Romano

16

AND suddenly there was with the angel a multitude of the heavenly host praising God, and saying, Glory to God in the highest, and on earth peace, good will toward men.

Host of angels (detail) from The Nativity by Gerard David

ND it came to pass, as the angels were
gone away from them into heaven, the
shepherds said one to another, Let us
now go even unto Bethlehem, and see this thing
which is come to pass, which the Lord hath made
known unto us. And they came with haste, and
found Mary, and Joseph, and the babe lying in a
manger. And when they had seen it, they made
known abroad the saying which was told them
concerning this child. And all they that heard it
wondered at those things which were told them by
the shepherds. But Mary kept all these things, and
pondered them in her heart. And the shepherds
returned, glorifying and praising God for all the
things that they had heard and seen, as it was
told unto them.

The Adoration of the Shepherds
by Gerard David

AND when eight days were accomplished for the circumcising of the child, his name was called JESUS, which was so named of the angel before he was conceived in the womb. And when the days of her purification according to the law of Moses were accomplished, they brought him to Jerusalem, to present him to the Lord; And to offer a sacrifice according to that which is said in the law of the Lord, A pair of turtledoves, or two young pigeons. And, behold, there was a man in Jerusalem, whose name was Simeon; and the same man was just and devout, waiting for the consolation of Israel: and the Holy Ghost was upon him. And it was revealed unto him by the Holy Ghost, that he should not see death, before he had seen the Lord's Christ. And he came by the Spirit into the temple: and when the parents brought in the child Jesus, to do for him after the custom of the law, Then took he him up in his arms, and blessed God, and said, Lord, now lettest thou thy servant depart in peace, according to thy word: For mine eyes have seen thy salvation, Which thou hast prepared before the face of all people; A light to lighten the Gentiles, and the glory of thy people Israel. And Joseph and his mother marvelled at those things which were spoken of him.

The Presentation
in the Temple (detail)
by Giovanni di Paolo

Now when Jesus was born in Bethlehem of Judaea in the days of Herod the king, behold, there came wise men from the east to Jerusalem, Saying, Where is he that is born King of the Jews? for we have seen his star in the east, and are come to worship him. When Herod the king had heard these things, he was troubled, and all Jerusalem with him. And when he had gathered all the chief priests and scribes of the people together, he demanded of them where Christ should be born. And they said unto him, In Bethlehem of Judaea: for thus it is written by the prophet, And thou Bethlehem, in the land of Juda, art not the least among the princes of Juda: for out of thee shall come a Governor, that shall rule my people Israel. Then Herod, when he had privily called the wise men, enquired of them diligently what time the star appeared. And he sent them to Bethlehem, and said, Go and search diligently for the young child; and when ye have found him, bring me word again, that I may come and worship him also. When they had heard the king, they departed; and, lo, the star, which they saw in the east, went before them, till it came and stood over where the young child was. When they saw the star, they rejoiced with exceeding great joy.

The Journey of the Magi
(detail) by Sassetta

ND when they were come into the house,
they saw the young child with Mary his
mother, and fell down, and worshipped
him: and when they had opened their treasures,
they presented unto him gifts; gold, and
frankincense, and myrrh. And being warned of God
in a dream that they should not return to Herod,
they departed into their own country another way.

The Adoration of the Magi
by Hieronymus Bosch

A N D when they were departed, behold, the angel of the Lord appeareth to Joseph in a dream, saying, Arise, and take the young child and his mother, and flee into Egypt, and be thou there until I bring thee word: for Herod will seek the young child to destroy him. When he arose, he took the young child and his mother by night, and departed into Egypt: And was there until the death of Herod: that it might be fulfilled which was spoken of the Lord by the prophet, saying, Out of Egypt have I called my son. But when Herod was dead, behold, an angel of the Lord appeareth in a dream to Joseph in Egypt, Saying, Arise, and take the young child and his mother, and go into the land of Israel: for they are dead which sought the young child's life. And he arose, and took the young child and his mother, and came into the land of Israel. But when he heard that Archelaus did reign in Judaea in the room of his father Herod, he was afraid to go thither: notwithstanding, being warned of God in a dream, he turned aside into the parts of Galilee: And he came and dwelt in a city called Nazareth: that it might be fulfilled which was spoken by the prophets, He shall be called a Nazarene.

The Flight into Egypt
by Adriaen Isenbrant

28

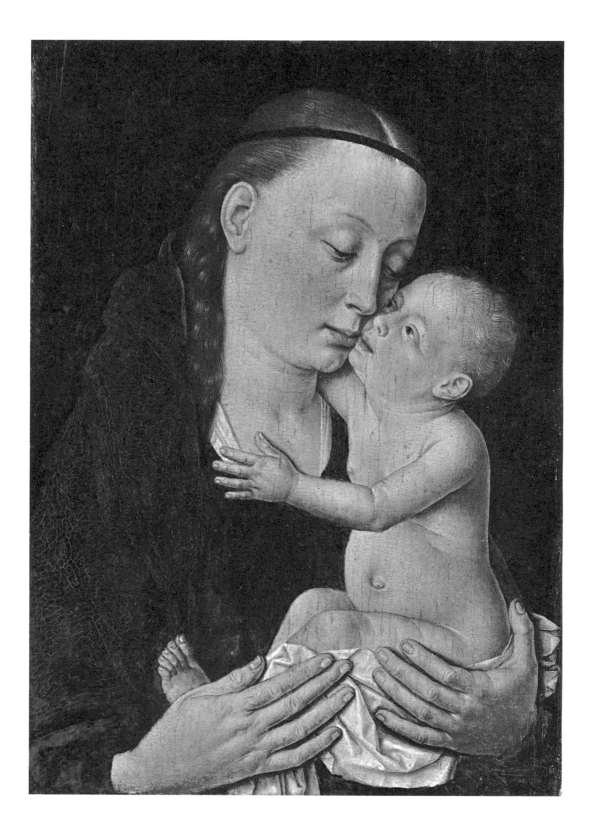

AND the child grew, and waxed strong in spirit, filled with wisdom: and the grace of God was upon him.

The Virgin and Child by Dieric Bouts

NOTES ON THE PAINTINGS

9 UNKNOWN PAINTER, northern France.
The Angel of the Annunciation, dated 1451. Tempera on wood, 45 x 31 inches. The Michael Friedsam Collection, 32.100.108

10 ROBERT CAMPIN, Flemish, active by 1406, died 1444.
The Annunciation, about 1425. Oil on wood, 25 3/16 x 24 7/8 inches. The Cloisters Collection, Purchase

13 FOLLOWER OF ROGIER VAN DER WEYDEN, Flemish.
The Visitation, second half of the 15th century. Tempera and oil on wood, 33 9/16 x 16 1/8 inches. The Cloisters Collection, Purchase, 49.109

14 WORKSHOP OF FRA ANGELICO, Italian, Florentine, 1387-1455.
The Nativity. Tempera on wood, 15 1/4 x 11 1/2 inches. Rogers Fund, 24.22

17 ANTONIAZZO ROMANO, Italian, Roman, active 1461-1508.
The Nativity. Tempera on wood, 11 1/2 x 26 1/2 inches. Rogers Fund, 06.1214

18 GERARD DAVID, Flemish, active by about 1484, died 1523.
The Nativity. Tempera and oil on canvas, 35 1/4 x 28 inches. The Jules S. Bache Collection, 49.7.20

21 GERARD DAVID, Flemish, active by about 1484, died 1523.
The Adoration of the Shepherds. Tempera and oil on wood, 18 3/4 x 13 1/2 inches. The Michael Friedsam Collection, 32.100.40

22 GIOVANNI DI PAOLO, Italian, Sienese, born 1402 or 1403, died about 1482.
The Presentation in the Temple. Tempera on wood, 15 1/2 x 18 1/8 inches. Gift of George Blumenthal, 41.100.4

25 SASSETTA (Stefano di Giovanni), Italian, Sienese, 1392-1450.
The Journey of the Magi. Tempera on wood, 8 1/2 x 11 5/8 inches. Bequest of Maitland F. Griggs, 43.98.1

26 HIERONYMUS BOSCH, Flemish, active by 1488, died 1516.
The Adoration of the Magi. Tempera and oil on wood, 28 x 22 1/4 inches. John Stewart Kennedy Fund, 13.26

29 ADRIAEN ISENBRANT, Flemish, active about 1510-1551.
The Flight into Egypt. Tempera and oil on wood, 10 3/4 x 3 1/2 inches. Frederick C. Hewitt Fund, 13.32

30 DIERIC BOUTS, Flemish, active by 1457, died 1475.
The Virgin and Child. Tempera and oil on wood, 8 1/2 x 6 1/2 inches. The Theodore M. Davis Collection. Bequest of Theodore M. Davis, 30.95.280

SOURCES OF THE WOODCUTS

Title page (upper right, center) *Meditationes* by Johannes de Turrecremata. Ulrich Han and Simon Nicolai Chardella, Rome, October 17, 1473. Harris Brisbane Dick Fund, 27.56

Title page (lower right) and 7, 19, 31 *Der beschlossen gart des Rosenkratz Marie* by Ulrich Pinder. Printed for the author, Nuremberg, October 9, 1505. Harris Brisbane Dick Fund, 31.83 (1)

8 *Missale Romanum.* Leon Pachel, Milan, April 16, 1499. Rogers Fund, 22.72.3

11, 12, 23 *Gaistliche usslegong des lebes Ihesu Cristi.* Johann Zainer, Ulm, about 1485. Harris Brisbane Dick Fund, 32.68.4

15 *Seelenwurzgarten.* Conrad Dinckmut, Ulm, July 26, 1483. Bequest of James Clark McGuire, 31.54.544

16, 28 *Das ist der Spiegel der Menschen behaltnis.* Peter Drach, Speier, 1478 or later. Harris Brisbane Dick Fund, 31.53

20 *Pistole, Lezzioni, et Vangeli.* i Giunti, Florence, 1565. Harris Brisbane Dick Fund, 25.30.21

24 *Leben der Heiligen Drei Könige,* by Johannes Hildesheimus. H. Knoblochtzer, Strassburg, about 1484. Bequest of James Clark McGuire, 31.54.439

27 Book cover for *Historia . . . Trium Regum,* by Johannes Hildesheimus. Rocciola, Modena, 1490. The Elisha Whittelsey Fund, 50.545